ALSO BY ANNE RENWICK

Black Sand and Blood

AN ELEMENTAL WEB STORY

ANNE RENWICK

To all the scientists specializing in bio-materials who looked at seashells and said, "I wonder if..."

THANK YOU TO...

Dj, my proofreader, who really wanted to know what happened to Dýri and Sóllilja—you'd not be reading this otherwise.

My husband, Jeff, for scrambling up muddy hillsides in Iceland with me for close-up views of the cave and hillock.

Sandra Sookoo, my wonderful editor who mercilessly ferrets out weaknesses and sets my work on a better course.

My mom and dad who instilled in me a love of both reading and travel.

Mr. Fox and his red pen.

CHAPTER ONE

Vik, Iceland
February 1885

"Were you ever going to tell me?" Resentful that she'd let him believe a lie—*for years*—Dýri heaved another shovel of heavy, wet sand over his shoulder onto the beach.

A month had passed since her fiancé had broken their engagement to wed another woman, and since the battle that had nearly cost Iceland its crown—a conflict in which she and Dýri had fought back to back. They'd yet to talk about why she'd let their friendship fade.

"Tell you what?" Sóllilja shot back. A casual reply, but her shoulders tightened, no doubt knowing she could no longer avoid this conversation.

She'd invited him on this expedition—it *was* their project—but deflected every question not directly related to their objective while refusing to meet his gaze. But his stubborn heart wouldn't let go of a hope that had quietly taken root, growing without any encouragement. Like a weed.

"That your engagement was nothing but a sham?" A well-bred huldufólk would let the topic drop. He was anything but that. "That you never intended to marry Val." Irritating, how she made him state the obvious. "That the whole ruse served no purpose other than to stop your father from pressuring you to marry some wealthy fae politician."

He'd pulled away. Respected boundaries that didn't exist. Maintained a tenuous friendship because he couldn't seem to let her go. Nor did she push him away. Was he a fool to think something still simmered between them?

He intended to find out tonight.

The sun had dropped behind the glacier an hour ago, but stopping meant the stench would only grow worse. Already, a blustery wind whipped the ocean into a froth, promising a night of icy snow and cutting gusts. A winter storm was blowing in their direction. If he stopped now, surging waves at high tide would bury the dead shell monster and he'd be digging the creature free from the black sand all over again tomorrow.

Or fighting to keep the carcass of the skeljaskrímsli from a certain cryptid hunter.

He didn't mind a good fight, but battling over rotting remains was not how he wished to spend his time with her.

And so they worked by the faint glowing lights of the lumitorcs they wore around their necks.

Even in death, the creature looked built for the deep—

armored, predatory, and never meant to leave the sea floor. Dense plates of overlapping shell glinted like wet stone in the moonlight, easily mistaken for a pile of rocks. Broad and muscular, it stood on short, powerful legs that ended in three curved, knife-like claws. An enormous hump rose from its back, tapering into a thick tail that ended in a stony, clubbed tip—a creature shaped by pressure, darkness, and hunger.

Before they could call it a night and seek shelter like sensible fae, he needed to drag the skeljaskrímsli's body two miles from Reynisfjara beach. For now, his heritage kept the worst of the cold from penetrating his thick skin, and Sóllilja wouldn't admit to discomfort if she lay on her deathbed with a cold steel arrow piercing her chest.

The many hours she spent training in the armory ensured she possessed a strength far beyond that of most fae, something he'd long admired. But—enticing curves aside— her petite frame meant she stood no chance at matching his strength or endurance. Dýri was simply taller, wider and in possession of a decided ancestral advantage.

"Not that it's any business of yours, but did you really think I'd trade this," she held up her bloody knife without looking up from her task, "for a life of silk-clad luxury and an endless tangle of political machinations when I could be working to protect our people?" She cut another armored plate from the fallen shell monster and threw it at his feet. "Who could rest easily in a comfortable chair beside a warm fire when they could spend a night in the field, covered in cold blood and wet sand, if it might save multiple fae lives?"

He snorted. On that, they agreed.

In the time he'd been digging to free the creature, she'd managed to cut loose some twenty armored plates from the fallen shell monster. By his estimate, over three hundred more remained. The farmer, who had shot and killed the *second* skeljaskrímsli to emerge from the sea in as many months, had saddled a horse and ridden straight to his pastor. The pastor—Dýri imagined him grim-lipped and stern—had sent a clockwork raven to peck at the closest huldufólk door behind a waterfall, one which happened to be Kvernufoss, demanding *something* be done.

Now, the fae weren't responsible for stopping random sea creatures from crawling up from the benthic depths, but Sóllilja had leapt at the chance to "dispose" of the carcass and to stockpile the nacre-coated shell plates for her project.

When word reached her, she'd convinced their mutual friend Val to drop them off at Vik while the rest of his crew continued northward on a journey to collect sunstone from the Helgustadir mine.

Which left them alone for a little under twenty-four hours. Time that Dýri intended to use to clear the air between them. Until now, their combined stubbornness and disinclination to be the first to admit their mutual attraction kept them hard at work, the better to avoid jagged emotions and spiky truths.

Well, that and the pressing matter of the ship looming on the horizon. From the shape of it, he'd wager his last horn of mead that it was *El Galeón Umbrío*. A rich Spaniard's toy. Equipped with every modern amenity, including a steam engine, but built to resemble the battle-scarred man-of-war ships that once crossed oceans in search of treasure, the better to haunt the waters and scare off anyone who dared challenge the captain's hunt for the unknown.

The vessel had dropped anchor behind the granite sea stacks as the sun set. With the water too rough to risk a crossing and the beach's habit of claiming lives with its sneaker waves, no tender boats had been launched. For now, the moonlit shadow of its hull represented nothing but a *potential* threat.

By whom? A Spanish cryptid hunter who went by the name of Lúgubre. Who else could possibly want this rotting heap of flesh?

Attending university like Val hadn't appealed to Dýri. Instead, he'd set off to see the world. When he'd heard about a group of men set to sail to Senegal in search of the fating'ho —a human-like creature with black fur and red eyes— curiosity lured him aboard. Which was how he'd found himself serving as a crew member aboard the man's ship.

At first, all had been... acceptable. But as the captain's hunger for fame deepened, so did his cruelty. Finding and studying cryptids was no longer enough. He began killing the adults and trapping their young, selling the offspring as exotic "pets." He harvested venom sacs, organs, and glands from living creatures, profiting piece by piece. Their suffering—physical and mental—he dismissed without a thought, locking them into cages that were far too small.

For a while, Dýri worked to sabotage the Spaniard's efforts. But when the man grew suspicious, Dýri and Lúgubre exchanged harsh words. All of them centered over the young House Nissi he'd enslaved. Trapped in Norway, dragged from his warm hearth and pressed into service to mend rigging, patch sails and caulk deck seams, the house spirit had been living in the ash bin next to the galley stove, living off sugar cubes, potato peels and bacon rinds.

The captain hadn't wished to part with the handy little Nissi, even after Dýri warned that once the spirit recovered from the shock of his imprisonment, he would retaliate in an angry rage. That food would rot and grow mold. That boilers would leak steam while rudders failed. That oil lamps would extinguish or tip over, putting them at risk for collision and fires.

Left with no choice but to terminate his employment, he'd liberated the Nissi at the next port and deserted ship. They'd almost escaped the galleon unnoticed. Alas, his bulk had cast too large a shadow. Shots had been fired while he descended a rope ladder to the dock with the Nissi clinging to his back. He'd had no choice but to fire back. If Lúgubre now walked with a limp, it was no one's fault but his own. As to the Nissi, the spirit was now happily ensconced in the bathhouse of a remote hot spring and treated with the respect due his kind.

Dýri was much happier working for his friend Val, even if it had involved him in a war against trolls under the influence of a madman. Only one thing in his life didn't sit right, and that was the small lie of omission he'd let his friends believe.

"It became my business," he forced himself to address the source of his current physical and emotional misery, "when your so-called oath nearly cost Val the airship on which I happen to work."

This time Sóllilja *did* look his way, with a gaze that could cut glass. She pointed the bloody blade at him. "That's a lie and you know it. Val dissolved our engagement without advance notice, not me. Say what you mean. Now that I'm a free woman, you're jealous. Do you dislike all the male attention thrown my way? Are you wondering how many men have woken up in my chamber this past month?"

He growled, not bothering to deny the truth, then took a step and dug deeper into the black sand, freeing the creature's foreleg.

"That's right." She sliced brutally into the shell monster's skin, angling her blade to loosen another plate. "You've no defense. You declined the opportunity to slide between my sheets, so keep your sneering judgment to yourself."

He tossed another shovelful of sand. Then another. And another. No one could raise his blood pressure faster than this woman.

Memories of that night haunted him. Stumbling down the long hallway after the party, half drunk and arm in arm, laughing as they propped each other up. Stopping at her rooms, planting a hand against the stone wall and leaning close as she unlocked her door.

She'd risen on tiptoes to drape her arms about his neck, trailed a kiss along his jawline before whispering, "Don't leave. Come to bed with me."

For years, he'd entertained fantasies of such an invitation. Before his brain could engage, his lips were on hers, his arms wrapped around her waist, and his foot kicked the door wide. With his body on fire, he'd contemplated stepping inside, slamming the door behind them and claiming her against its rough wooden surface, saving any soft horizontal locations for later.

And wasn't that the problem, thinking? His stomach had roiled as he'd recalled all the reasons they couldn't be together. Without warning, he'd dropped her back on her heels. "No, Sóllilja, we can't." Offering no explanation, he'd pushed her inside, closed her door and walked away.

After that night, their friendship grew uncomfortable, fading until nothing remained between them save her attempts to perfect nacreweft, a lightweight woven armor. He'd leave shells from exotic locations at her door. She'd process them, wet-spin a new spool of thread, nålbind a new fabric swatch. The resultant fabric sample—tattered, torn or slashed—would arrive by clockwork raven along with notes as to how this latest version had failed the tests.

And so it went, year after year. A cycle of shells, thread, and failure. The small ritual the only tether that still bound them to each other. Whatever friendship they'd once shared had been ground down into a hollow exchange. He left pieces of his heart at her threshold. She returned nothing but shreds.

It wasn't until he'd delivered a few armored plates from a dead shell monster that she'd hit upon a winning formula. A small, perfectly intact swatch had arrived. The winning source of shell? A sea monster that rarely ventured ashore.

He'd been impressed when she'd demonstrated how the gloves she'd constructed from nacreweft deflected even the sharp tip of her blade. Gloves she now wore to protect her hands from the jagged edges of the creature's armored plates.

Dýri threw aside his shovel and wrapped a chain around the shell monster's ankle. Time to pull the creature free and drag it elsewhere.

She threw another bloody nacre plate in his direction.

Enough. Cards on the table. "I turned down your drunken offer of a *single* night's amusement."

"Why?" She pinned her gloved hands on her hips and glared at him. Wild and beautiful in her fury, covered in blood and gore, finally ready to admit they had unfinished business. "There's no shame in a night's pleasure."

"Agreed," he snapped. "But I wanted more."

Knife in hand, she stomped up the slope of the wet sand until they were nose to nose. "And what kept you from that?"

He scowled. "You enjoy fighting trolls."

Confusion rippled across her face. "What has that to do with anything?"

The admission scraped from his throat. "I am one."

CHAPTER TWO

His words didn't register for a moment. "What do you mean?" Her eyebrows drew together. She straightened, abandoning her task of packing the armored plates into a crate. Dýri had always lived in the mountain with all the other huldufólk. They'd grown up side by side. "You're *not* a troll."

"Part," he replied. "My grandmother lives in a cave near the Dimmuborgir lava fields."

"In Mývatn?" The words fell dumbly from her lips. "*She's* a troll?"

Though the pain of admitting such contorted his features, he nodded. "You've dedicated your life to fighting trolls, sneering at their stupidity, mocking their lifestyle."

Her breath left her in a short, stunned laugh. It wasn't funny, but it was that or scream. Of all the things she'd expected to hear from him tonight, this wasn't one of them. The echoes of the battle they'd fought still rang in her ears.

She stared at him, at a familiar face she'd known her entire life. Her friend, the man she'd lusted after for years. Part troll. He wasn't supposed to be one of *them*.

Her mouth opened, closed. "You—" She swallowed hard. "You should have told me."

He flinched.

She waited for revulsion to hit. But nothing happened. This was *Dýri*. "But... but you were raised in the mountain? With elves?"

"My mother was born a weakling, sent to my father to be raised by the fae side of the family." He tilted his head and offered her a wry grin. "Did you never wonder why the Yule cat visited me every winter? Why my mother was so fast to nålbind a new sweater for me each and every December, insisting I wear it while Jólakötturinn was on the prowl? She knew my grandmother would send her cat to look in on me."

That explained much. A smile tugged at the corner of her lips. He'd hated those stifling, itchy garments. Complained endlessly. But wore them, nonetheless. At least until they'd all reached the hot spring, where he'd yank the sweater over his head and throw it on the stones surrounding the pool.

She'd looked forward to his misery every winter. To the nights when their group of friends snuck out on a stormy winter's night, slipping and sliding down the mountain pathway to the hot spring. Not so much because Dýri suffered wearing the scratchy wool, but because those evenings spent soaking in the hot water presented her with the glorious view of his bare chest with all his muscles flexing and shifting beneath his bronzed skin. Easier to disguise her stares as steam rose around them.

He'd always been the biggest and the strongest of their friends. Heredity? Likely. She'd often wondered if *all* of him was so very large and thick. Heat crept into her cheeks as she recalled the drunken night when she'd decided to find out. His kiss burned in her memory. As did his sudden and sharp rejection.

"I don't hate trolls as a general principle." A partial retraction. Her stomach squeezed at the thought of the harsh words she'd spoken about the jötunn over the years. "Only those that try to kill us."

Doubtful, he flattened his lips. "Please. Do me a favor and don't lie."

"Fine. I was jealous."

His eyebrows lifted. "Jealous?"

"Of the field training you and Val received." An admission that emerged on a grumble. "Even Hildur was allowed out onto the lava fields to practice sword fighting, archery, knives at close quarters. While I was trapped at home and subjected to etiquette and dance lessons." She jabbed a finger into his chest. Into massive, rock-hard muscles she'd not laid eyes on in years. Her hands ached to explore, but she had no right to touch him, not in such a manner. "I talked tough when you returned, bragging about how I was just as handy with a sword as all of you when I could barely snatch a few hours a week in the armory. I couldn't keep up. Still can't."

His gaze swept over her body as he stared at her with quiet admiration. "No one expected that of you."

Warmth rushed over her.

Behind him stretched the dark sea, its frothy whitecaps marking where water met land. Harsh. Strong. Unyielding. Exactly like him. Was there any hope of winning his forgiveness?

"*I* expected it of *me.*" She'd worked hard to hone her skills, to strengthen her arms to withstand his blows. Val's and Hildur's too. But only one man held her complete focus. Heat rose to her face. "Baiting you into testing my claims, into crossing swords in mock battle was the only time I had you to myself."

For all the good it had done. She'd been left behind anyway when her friends leapt aboard the airship, waved and sailed off. That had been part of the bargain made with her father—he would fund the airborne research vessel, but only if she stayed in the mountain until they married. A wedding postponed for years, as theirs was a contractual engagement that neither of them intended to end before a priest.

A wicked gust of icy wind snatched at Dýri's hair. The sharp planes of his chiseled face and the dark shadows of a beard that bristled along his jawline were familiar. But his time aboard an airship had weathered him. His shoulders were broader. His arms thicker. His thighs sturdier.

She swallowed as something low in her stomach fluttered. Covered in blood and gore, wearing rough trousers and an old tunic, her hair—initially braided—was a knotted, disgusting mess. But he didn't back away from her, didn't flinch. If anything, his glittering eyes dared her to come closer.

Needling her had been one of his favorite pastimes. Teasing her to the boiling point when her emotions would burst free. He'd only laughed as she pummeled his chest, pinched his arm or yelled in his ear. Something she loved about him.

Loved. Not lust. Though there was plenty of that as well. And on one drunken night, with her inhibitions lowered, she'd invited him to her bed.

He'd declined.

After that, he'd avoided her. Life moved on. One thing led to another and, when her father pressured her to marry a diplomat, she'd conspired with Val. A real engagement, but never a marriage. To be dissolved when one of them wished to marry another. She was freed from societal expectations, and Val won the funds to launch his airship. Unfortunately, he'd also recruited every last one of their mutual friends as crew before floating away to distant lands.

But now that was over. Val had a wife, and Sóllilja was free.

She narrowed her eyes. "Are you asking me if I find your heritage repulsive?"

He tipped his head. "Do you?"

"No! There's not an offensive thing about you. If anything—" She broke off. "Is this your method of initiating a courtship?" She waved her knife over the dead skeljaskrímsli.

"Helping me harvest nacre armor plates before this Lúgubre person swoops in and runs off with a rare Icelandic beast?"

He leaned close, smirking at the frustrated confusion of her words, and tucked a lock of fluttering hair behind her ear. A useless gesture—the wind would whip it free momentarily. "Do you want it to be?"

"I—" She broke off, pondering the ramifications of declaring herself.

Marriage to Dýri?

Her younger self had believed it impossible, if only because his family ranked far lower than hers. Now that she knew he was part troll? Internally, she cringed at the inevitable reaction of her parents. They would know his family's history.

But she was older, wiser and less averse to conflict. Her life was what she made of it. Did she want him? Yes. Did he want her?

His gaze dropped to her lips, and that was all the encouragement she needed.

Leaning forward, she pressed her mouth to his. A soft invitation. One he accepted without hesitation. Catching her jaw with sand-dusted fingers, he tipped her face, finding the perfect angle to deepen their kiss. A move that sent sparks dancing along her skin.

A low growl rumbled from his throat, and she parted her lips, meeting his tongue to tangle in a long-denied, breath-stealing reckoning of suppressed desire. His warmth tasted like everything missing from her life, sweet and spicy with a hint of his favorite indulgence, salted caramel.

He stepped closer, wrapped an arm about her waist and yanked her against him. A gesture she didn't dare echo, given the disastrous state of her gloved hands. Instead, she rose up on her toes, a silent entreaty for more. For so, so much more.

But then his mouth left hers.

"Let me know." He tapped her on the nose. "When you figure it out."

And then he was gone, once more bent over the shell monster's forelimb, tightening the chain around its ankle and hooking it to the sand walker, equipment designed to drag heavy boats—not creatures—out of the water and across sand. With the ease of great strength, he wound the spring mechanism. Then, with the flip of a lever, a winch dragged the partly buried sea monster out of the sand and onto the back half of the skid sled partly loaded with crates—only one of which she'd managed to fill with the creature's nacre plates.

All while she stood there holding a bloody knife trying to find her footing on the ever-shifting sands of her life as icy snow lashed at the exposed skin of her face. She'd kissed Dýri. He'd kissed her back.

"Get a move on!" With the creature secured, he flipped another lever, and the sand walker flexed its limbs and pulled, moving the entirety of their operation across the wave-washed beach. "Is there a problem?"

She shook her head, but her feet refused to move. Did she want him? A ridiculous question. She'd wanted him for years. But marriage? If she wasn't horribly mistaken, he'd all but proposed. Hope froze her where she stood.

For the first time in ages, she indulged in the idea of a life with him, together. A scary prospect, allowing such thoughts to escape the realms of fantasy. Could she toss aside all the expectations and privileges of fae society and allow herself to snatch at the chance for love?

Though a rough cave was anything but romantic, a long night stretched in front of them where they would be completely alone.

Dýri flashed her a knowing smile, then turned away to guide the walker across the dark beach.

They'd made plans to shelter overnight in a cave located some two miles west of Reynisfjara beach. There, come daybreak, the airship would pick them up on its return flight.

The hope was that, after dragging the sea creature out of the intertidal zone to a new location, the incoming storm would erase their tracts and leave the cryptid hunter and his crew futilely digging come morning as they searched for a shell monster they were certain was only a few feet beneath the black sand.

Bending, she snatched up the two nacre plates and clutched them to her chest. The armor had failed to protect the skeljaskrímsli, and she doubted the disarticulated scales would do much to safeguard her own heart.

Not if Dýri decided to try cracking its shell.

CHAPTER THREE

Once the shock of his revelation wore off, Sóllilja quickly caught up to him, running and jumping onto the dead carcass, kneeling on its back as she wielded her sharp knife to pry off yet more nacre plates while they were in motion. An interesting avoidance tactic, but there was time later for a long, late-night conversation once they reached Loftsalahellir Cave.

After years of avoiding the topic, he'd not only announced long-standing romantic interest, but a desire to see it end in matrimony. A woman deserved a chance to ponder the consequences of binding herself to a man like him.

Thunk. Clunk. Thud. One after another armored scale landed in the storage crates.

For the first mile, the mechanized sand walker encountered no difficulties dragging the skeljaskrímsli-loaded skid sled over smooth sand. Then, at the edge of the pond—an inlet, really—he stopped to attach and inflate the skid buoys. There, he'd glanced up to find she'd filled another two crates.

He'd rowed them across the inlet. Even then, Sóllilja didn't slide from the back of the beast to join him. No, she sat astride the creature's back, blonde strands of hair flying about her face in the lashing wind and whipping snow, looking like Skadi, the Norse goddess of the hunt.

Lust stirred. He tamped it down. The journey wasn't over, and she wouldn't rest until all the nacre was harvested.

This past century, huldufólk had mostly lived a quiet existence, tucked inside their mountain home, tending to the traditional agricultural and livestock fields while adding more erudite scientific pursuits such as tapping into Iceland's vast stores of geothermal power. More recently, they'd become inextricably entangled with Iceland's bid for independence from Denmark.

After the recent Battle of the Trolls, when a madman enslaved a number of his distant relatives in an attempt to steal the throne, huldufólk guards would be embedded in the king's entourage, making their efforts to develop a lightweight armor that offered protection without sacrificing mobility of particular interest.

The threads from which she'd woven her earliest prototypes had possessed a fatal flaw. When exposed to damp weather, the fibers proved hydrophilic, attracting moisture. The swollen filaments grew weak, losing all tensile strength. Wet and soggy armor offered no protection.

Then a skeljaskrímsli washed up on one of Iceland's black sand beaches. Curious if the armored plates of a vertebrate differed from those of mollusks, he'd harvested a handful of the armored plates and delivered them to Sóllilja, hoping this time something would be different.

And it was. Though he'd barely understood her ramblings about trace elements and the different organic matrix that constituted the skeljaskrímsli's nacre, the key thing was that the fibers she spun were stronger, iridescent and—even better—water resistant.

They'd only lacked a large enough source of the raw material.

So when reports of another skeljaskrímsli reached their ears, Sóllilja sprang into action, begging a ride aboard an airship, to harvest the armored plates before the sea reclaimed the creature's body.

But now competition threatened, which was why her efforts to strip the scales from the beast resumed the moment their skids hit the far side of the inlet, as Dýri engaged the mechanical sand walker to haul their cargo onto the sand and gravelly terrain below the looming Hjörleifshöfði mountain. Carved into this lava formation was the cave that would serve as tonight's campground.

Once again, he deployed the sand walker, but only long enough to drag them a few feet from the brackish water.

There, he disengaged the mechanism, disassembled the walker, and packed it away. That done, he turned his efforts to organizing the nacre plates Sóllilja had haphazardly tossed into empty crates. Packed tightly, the collected scales required only three crates, not four, leaving several still available for stockpiling more of the special nacre. He nailed their lids in place, readying them for transport aboard the airship.

The sound of his hammer alerted Sóllilja to their lack of movement.

"Is this as far as we can go?" Frowning, she paused her efforts and turned to stare over her shoulder, squinting across the inlet and Reynisfjara beach to where distant basalt stacks rose from the surf.

Not that they—or *El Galeón Umbrío*—were visible at this distance in a snowstorm.

"We can't see them. They can't see us. Not until the storm abates, and the sun rises." He pulled a knife from the sheath at his hip and eyeballed the dead monster, calculating how to remove the remaining scales in as short a time as possible. "But we won't stop until we're done and ready to dispose of the evidence."

He stalked over to the creature's shoulder and slid his blade beneath a plate, ignoring the wet, sucking sound that met his ears. This wasn't the first animal he'd butchered, though it was the first shell monster. After a few wrong maneuvers, he figured it out. The trick was to find the connective tissue, slipping the knife's edge just above the bone to sever the sinewy ligaments that stitched the armor to the muscle below.

The blade rasped across the calcified ridges of the nacre scales, then the entire plate popped free with a jerk. Coppery blood spread over the skin of his wrist, cold and clotted, like spoiled milk. He wiped his arm on his tunic and carried on.

Each scale peeled off like a giant toenail, thick as a slate roof tile and just as hard. The stench emanating from the dead monster intensified as they exposed muscle blackened with decay and sulfurous pockets of gas hidden beneath the creature's skin.

One after another, he tossed scales onto the ground. The growing pile brought to mind a grotesque disassembled mosaic.

For hours they slogged away at the task, working as the snowstorm whipped around them. Every so often, Dýri would stop, load a crate, and nail down the lid before once again wielding his knife.

Finally, the entirety of the creature's back—the largest of the armored plates—had been stripped bare, and the single crate still open was more than half full. Though he barely felt the cold—there were perks to his troll heredity—Sóllilja had begun to fumble, her fingers clumsy from the chill. The nacreweft gloves she wore protected her hands from cuts, not the falling temperature. She needed to stop, to rest, to warm up.

He rolled his shoulders, drew in a breath of icy air. Snow was accumulating. "We should call it a night." Take advantage of the storm's assistance in destroying signs of their presence.

She glanced at the half-empty crate and shook her head. "The belly scutes are smaller and softer. Their composition will be different and—"

"We'll fill the last of the crate with them." With her mind

fixed upon an incomplete task, there would be no wooing her.

That earned him a smile. If one tinged with exhaustion. "Help me roll the skeljaskrímsli?"

They braced their backs against the slick flank of the monster and heaved, boots slipping in the blood-drenched sand. The creature's bulk resisted, but bit by bit, they shifted its mass enough for gravity and the slight slope to take over.

With a final shove, the shell monster rolled. And flopped belly up with a thunderous wet *thump*, displacing brackish water and wet sand. Half in and half out of the pond.

Excellent.

"We fill the remaining crate, then push the skeljaskrímsli into the water," he said. "It's better that Lúgubre not know we were here."

She frowned, examining his plan for flaws "Won't the carcass float?"

"Not for a few days." Not while it was still relatively fresh. Once the gases built up, the belly would bloat, and it would rise. Slowly and reluctantly. "By then, Odin willing, we'll be long gone."

They stood in silence a moment. Then the knives came out again.

They'd only peeled away a few nacre scutes from the creature's stomach when a loud hiss met his ears. He looked to find Sóllilja clutching her hand.

"What happened?" Words that were more a demand than a question.

"Nothing but a small nick." Her face paled. "I'm fine."

He grabbed her hand. *Hel.* Fresh blood welled upward through a tear along the seam of her nålbound nacreweft gloves. He lifted an eyebrow.

"I used sinew to sew the fabric together," she admitted, vexed. "There wasn't enough thread left on the spool to finish them properly."

The cut wasn't long, but it *was* deep. Had the creature's blood mixed with hers? His pulse jumped with concern. Its acidity might erode her flesh. He dug into their supplies. Grabbing a box of sodium bicarbonate, he ripped off the lid and shook the powder over the cut, neutralizing any threat. "You're done." He snatched her blade away. He'd not let her risk further damage. "Wash up." He tipped his head at the inlet pond. "Then wrap it. The wound needs suturing."

Grimacing, she turned to the crates. "As soon as I pack the scutes."

"I'll finish here." He fixed her with a hard stare, daring her to contradict what was an unmistakable order. With a sigh, she moved to obey. A first.

He loaded the belly scales with brutal efficiency. Driving a final nail into the lid of the last crate, he wiped their blades clean and stowed all tools. With the skid sled's runners pointed toward their cave and its chains hitched to the reassembled walker, one last task remained.

Back against the skeljaskrímsli, he heaved, shifting it into the inlet until it half floated in the water. With a final shove, the beast rolled, tumbling down a slope of submerged rocks and sand, disappearing into a watery grave.

CHAPTER FOUR

Frigg *and* Hel. The pain was sharp, jagged and throbbing, even after she knotted a clean rag tightly around the wound.

Her blade had cut near to the bone. Not through the nålbound nacreweft fabric, but through the sinew she'd used to join the seams. She'd run out of nacreweft thread when she'd sewn these gloves and had resorted to traditional materials. Her mistake.

But—a grim smile pulled at the corner of her mouth—it *was* proof of concept.

Next time, she'd do better. And there would be a next time, thanks to the ten large crates of nacre-armored plates they'd harvested from the dead skeljaskrímsli. Enough that she might even surrender a few to the scientists in hopes they could re-create the strange nacre in a laboratory setting so there'd be no further need to skin—disarticulate—any more shell monsters.

Splash!

She looked up as Dýri rolled the creature's carcass into the inlet. Set in motion, it tumbled downward, disappearing under the dark water. Into near-freezing water.

The only water available to wash the blood and gore from her skin and clothing. A hand lifted to her wind-blown hair—her hat long since lost to the storm—informed her it was a tangled mess.

Dýri stalked to her side and waved uphill. "Let's head for the cave." A dangerous smile stretched his lips wide. "With luck, supplies await us."

Her eyebrows rose. "Supplies?"

"I sent a raven ahead with a pouch of coins and a list of provisions. If the farmer knows what's good for him, our night in Loftsalahellir cave will be a comfortable one."

She ought to have thought of such a measure instead of resigning herself to a night wrapped in nothing more than a single blanket with a rock for her pillow. And here he was, taking care of her. Making it impossible to keep her heart steady and her mind clear.

Her mood brightened. Likely he'd threatened the man, but she found it hard to worry under current circumstances. "Food? Water? Wood?"

"All of those." His eyes danced. "And more."

More? Excellent. The cave wasn't far. Just up the hill. Knowing this would be disgusting work, they'd packed a change of clothing. And she wasn't crawling into bed with the remains of butchering clinging to her hair.

Though, from the sly look upon Dýri's face and his

earlier questions, sleep was the last thing on his mind. Would he finally act on their attraction after years of simmering and stewing and throwing her heated glances during her sham engagement? Take it further than a single kiss?

She was a bloody mess, but the way he looked at her made her ache to be touched. It would make all this self-inflicted torture worth it. She glanced at the dark, cold water. Wrapped in his arms, she'd soon be more than warm enough. But she refused to step into his embrace in her current state.

"Good." With numb fingers she worked the buttons of her sheepskin coat free, hauled the garment from her shoulders, and tossed it atop the crates. "Let's rinse off."

Enjoying his slack-jawed stare, she walked into the freezing water. For a moment, her lungs rebelled at the shock, refusing to draw breath, even though she was no more than waist deep.

Water sloshed near her. "Have you lost your mind?"

But he reached for her too late. Bent at the hip, she plunged her head into the icy water and scrubbed at her scalp with her fingertips—save for the one she curled into her palm. She tossed her head back, flinging an arc of drops into the air as icicles crystalized in her hair.

Instantly, she started shivering. "Tell me this farmer kindled a fire?"

"You're insane."

Her teeth chattered as she grinned. "The reason you love me?"

He rolled his eyes, then grabbed her shoulders, turned her about and pointed. "March. Straight up that hill. You'll sense a path, a groove in the landscape. Leave everything as it is. I'll be right behind you."

As commanded, something to which she was not accustomed as head of all huldufólk guards, she strode from the water and focused all her remaining energy on grabbing a wool blanket from her travel chest, wrapping it about her shoulders and trudging up the hillside.

A few steps into her effort, she risked turning around for a moment. Long enough to catch a glimpse of Dýri, now freshly scrubbed himself, emerging from the water barechested, his tattoos on full display. Her jaw dropped. Yes, at the sight of so much bare skin carelessly exposed to freezing temperatures, but also at the ripple of muscles across his torso. There were new twists of vines tattooed upon his chest to admire, true, but the boy she remembered from the hot spring was gone. Time and trial had honed his physique so sharply, she couldn't help but wonder if the gods had shaped it themselves.

Dýri caught her staring and locked eyes with her, a carnal gaze that promised to ruin her for all other men, if only she agreed to his terms.

He wasn't looking for a single night's fun. Nor for a succession of secret trysts. But marriage?

For too many years, Dýri had kept her at a solid arm's length, their only interaction the occasional discussions about the structural integrity of the latest iteration of nacreweft and what might, possibly, be done to improve it.

Her fault, given she'd initiated a sham engagement with a mutual friend.

But when Val cried off—having married another woman —Dýri had begun turning up, bumping into her in the hallways. Standing by the runestone in the central courtyard to discuss with the mountain council how to handle the huldufólk's new, tentative alliance with Grýla's trolls.

Not a single romantic overture. She'd all but given up hope.

The only time he'd approached her directly was to hand her five armored plates from a shell monster, the first one to appear on Vik's beaches in years, to suggest they test the effectiveness of this creature's nacre.

Miraculously, the new formulation had worked. Repelling water. Retaining tensile strength under damp conditions. And, most unexpectedly, the wet-spun threads had shimmered and shifted creating an optical illusion that, when woven into cloth, encouraged people to overlook the wearer. A bonus for those guards who would be assigned to work with humans. Much as the huldufólk had agreed to an integrated security detail for the Icelandic court, they did not wish for attention. Anything that concealed the difference between human and fae would be welcome.

Alas, the five plates—dissolved and reconstituted—had barely produced enough thread for three tunics. She'd kept the remnants, nålbinding the remaining thread into gloves, but sewing the seams with a bone needle and a length of fine sinew. Something her pulsing finger reminded her of with each heartbeat.

Then word arrived that another skeljaskrímsli had been shot.

While they worked, a steady fall had coated the shore with a fresh layer of snow—and it was still coming down fast and furious. Snow they would need to hide their tracks if they wished to spend a peaceful night alone in a cave.

She snorted. Knowing them, their time together would be anything but peaceful. A thought that warmed her to her very core and hurried her steps onto a rut carved into the earth by thousands of prior footsteps. After so many years of denying themselves each other, what might all their hunger erupt into when it finally broke free? Her thoughts spun, each one of them circling back to his strength, to what it might feel like unleashed.

Behind her, the walker ground into motion, hauling the skid sled with its many crates partway up the rock-strewn slope, tucking it beside a rocky outcropping not far from the water's edge. Covered with a canvas tarp, freshly fallen snow would all but conceal its location.

As she hiked up the hill, her steps grew heavy and slow. Stupid, ignoring the laws of thermodynamics to plunge her head into icy water, but she'd do it again without regrets.

Finally, the triangular black maw of the cave opened before her. The lumitorc that hung about her neck cast a faint blue-white light into the cavern and onto its walls. Not a particularly large space, but it was halfway up a mountain and several miles removed from the beach where the cryptid hunters would search for a dead shell monster come morning.

With any luck, she and Dýri would climb aboard their

ride home at first light, departing long before Lúgubre and his men set foot on sand.

The farmer had delivered supplies as promised. Three stoneware jugs, a small iron cauldron, and a short stack of wood and a bundle of kindling rested beside a large wicker basket. Tucked inside were paper-wrapped provisions and a handful of beeswax candles. Next to the basket was a pile of thick sheepskins—a makeshift mattress.

Her heart gave a great thud.

Behind her, dark clouds and blowing snow blotted out the night sky. Until the storm blew over, a fire was a risk she was willing to take. She tossed aside her blanket. With trembling fingers, she dug a shallow depression into the sandy gravel and set about building a campfire. Sparks flew as she struck flint to iron—most of them missing the kindling by an embarrassing margin—but finally one caught.

Dýri stepped into the cave, bare-chested. Without a word, he pushed her—broad hands on hips—onto a nearby rock. She sat watching dumbly as he stacked wood atop the growing fire. In mere moments, he was pouring water into the cauldron, where it hung from an iron tripod over the flames.

"Boots off, you madwoman." His fingers deftly unlaced her footwear. "There was no need for an icy plunge." One after the other, he threw aside her boots and cupped her frozen feet in his palms. A tingling warmth spread across her skin. "Put your hands on my chest."

She complied, sighing with relief. "How are you still warm?"

He shrugged. "Always have been." Snatching up her hand, he examined her bandage. "How bad is it?"

"It'll wait a bit."

"Good." Tugging at her trousers, he lifted an eyebrow. "Because your clothes all need to come off. Now. Am I turning my back?"

A rusty laugh escaped her throat. "Do you want to?"

He ran a hand up her leg, over her thigh, then curved across her hip until his thumb brushed over the buckle of her belt. Her muscles went taut beneath his touch, every nerve straining toward that single point where his thumb rested. With deft fingers, he freed the clasp. The leather strip—and everything clipped to it—fell to the ground.

"No. No more games, Sóllilja. I want you. I want *us*."

She swallowed. "I can't promise—"

"More than tonight." He jerked a nod. "So you say, but I'm done waiting. Tell me you want this too, and I'll have you pressed against me, skin to skin, all hot and bothered before you can string a full sentence together."

Locking her gaze on the dark pools of his eyes, she smoothed her hands over the thick muscle of his shoulders and whispered. "Gods, I want—"

His arm shot under her knees as his other wrapped around her waist. Before she'd blinked twice, he'd carried her to the back of the cave and set her feet upon her discarded blanket, facing away. In moments, her corset fell loose. "Hands up." He gripped the hem of her shirt and pulled it over her head.

Where he tossed the garment failed to register, for the

smooth skin of her back pressed against the hard planes of his chest as his hand fanned upward over her ribcage, fingers bumping against the underside of her breast. He drew aside damp hair and nipped her neck. "I'm not intending to be gentle, not this time, not after years of pent-up frustration. If that's a problem, tell me." His thumbs hooked over her waistband. "Because we can stop."

His hands left her skin.

"Don't you dare." She shoved her loose leggings to the ground and nudged her hips back against his erection.

With a low laugh, he pushed her slightly away. But before she could protest, his belt buckle jangled and his trousers fell away.

Then he was back. On a groan, he palmed a breast but slid his other hand over her mound where his fingers found her warm and wet. Rough fingertips played with her erect nipple; others circled the tight bundle of nerves between her legs. Stroking. Pinching. Teasing. All while he ground against her buttocks.

Close. She was so very close. But she wanted him in her, wanted him to feel her clench around him as she climaxed. Wanted to watch his face as his careful control shattered.

"Dýri." Spinning, she wrapped her arms around his neck and drew his mouth to hers, desperate for the feel of his lips fused to hers. Promising herself more of this later, she pulled away. Their eyes locked. She saw longing and love. And lust unleashed. The future she wanted. She wrapped a leg about his hip. His thick length pulsed against her wetness. "Take me standing. I want us together. Now."

With a growl, he cupped her arse and hauled her from the ground. *Freyja*, she loved his raw strength. The moment his tip was at her entrance, he surged forward with a feral cry and plunged deep into her. Stretching her, filling her, leaving her gasping for air.

"Sóllilja?" A hesitant note.

"More." She sank her teeth into his shoulder, urging him to hurry.

GODS. He'd dreamt of this for ages.

He hooked an arm under her thigh and clasped the opposite buttock with a single hand. He planted the other on the stone wall behind her. Her arms around his neck, legs clasping his hips. Soft breasts crushed against his hard chest. Her tight channel squeezing his length.

For a moment, he rocked. Letting her body adjust. Because a primitive part of his brain, urged onward by the bite of her mouth, intended to claim her hard and fast. Slow would be for next time. On the thick pile of sheepskins.

Fingers slid along his scalp. Flexed. Pulled at the roots of his hair. "Dýri!" She twisted in his arms. "Move!"

After all these years of torturing each other, her impatience was wickedly gratifying. And no less sharp-edged than his own.

He slid away, then drove his hips forward in a hard and deep thrust.

"Yes," her fingernails dug into his skin, exactly the encouragement he wanted.

Over and again, he surged into her. Watched her small, perfect breasts bounce as a flush rose to her cheeks. They were so close, so very close to achieving perfection. But the angle...

—>—✦—<—

She was close. So achingly close, but not quite—

Without warning, Dýri pushed off the wall and turned. As his back dropped against the cave wall, he shifted his grip. With his forearms braced beneath her spread thighs, he gripped the flare of her hip bones, fingers digging deep. The raw strength with which he yanked her to him as he thrust upward made her cry out as stars appeared in the corner of her vision.

"Oh, my gods!" Her screams sparked encouragement, for his next thrust was even harder, and the angle reached some deep place inside her that flared a desire like she'd never felt before. "Yes!"

Eyes locked on hers, he repeated the movement. Again. And again. Tension wound through her body—tighter and tighter—until it snapped. She cried out at the sudden release as he drove impossibly deep. Once. Twice. Then, with a guttural groan, he pulsed inside her, surrendering to the same fiery, all-consuming climax.

Their bodies stilled, breaths ragged. He rested his forehead against hers and, for a moment, neither of them moved.

Joined as one, she whispered, "We were fools to wait so long."

His answering laugh rumbled through her chest. "With diligence, we can make up for lost time."

She glanced at the makeshift bed. A rush of heat pooled low in her belly. A cave and an entire night to themselves. What could be better? She shot him a heated look, daring him to deliver on that promise. "Beginning tonight?"

"Tonight." The rasp of his voice sent a rush of heat down her spine. He lifted her injured hand and pressed a kiss to her palm. "As soon as we clean and stitch the gash."

CHAPTER FIVE

Inside the cave, the fire had chased away the winter night's chill as it warmed water. As long as the wind lashed and snow scoured the mountainside, they were safe. The outside world couldn't reach them. He'd feared it would never allow them this moment. But now, with their long-denied desires laid bare, he'd surrendered to instinct—to her—and finally, *finally* claimed her as his own.

Soft and warm in his arms, nuzzling his neck, Sóllilja wanted more. But her heart was still guarded. When this night ended, would she turn him away? Social rank mattered among the huldufólk. A physical relationship between them would be tolerated, but one involving committed vows would invite cold shoulders and quiet contempt.

Nothing would change for him. He was accustomed to veiled insults, to comments about his size, his strength, and half-whispered theories about who—or what—his father had married. But for Sóllilja? Raised in a world of comfort and status, wrapped in silk and handed silver spoons, binding herself to a man such as him meant she risked everything.

Her parents might disown her. The council might revoke her seat, remove her as head guard and deny them access to the laboratories, scientists and technology needed to produce nacreweft fabric at scale. Would she risk it all for *him*? Could he even ask that of her?

Warm and clean and dry, she sat naked on the generous pile of sheepskins he'd specifically instructed the farmer to deliver. He'd planned this seduction. Hoped for more beyond a single night, for more than an extended affair. Was it selfish to ask for more?

Sóllilja held her hand aloft, averting her eyes as he studied the gash in her finger. "Do it fast."

"No." He threaded the sharkskin thread through the eye of a tiny needle. His fingers were big—he was no seamstress or surgeon—but, for her, he would do this and *do it well*. "All you need are two small stitches. This will be no worse than the ethanol."

She groaned.

Dropping onto a rock beside the three bright candles that stood in pools of wax, he pinned her hand between his knees and squinted. "Don't move."

Slowly, carefully, he pierced the flesh on one side of the cut, then the other, and drew the two halves together. Sóllilja hissed through clenched teeth but held still. One more time, he drew the steel needle through her skin, then tied a perfect knot. He cut the thread. "Done."

Another splash of ethanol and a clean gauze bandage

completed the task. Then he doused the campfire. Better safe than sorry. A quick scan of the cave—all supplies stowed and tucked into shadows, boots and dry clothing resting bedside, sword, battle-axe and other assorted blades within an arm's reach—reassured him they were prepared for intruders. Free to enjoy the flicker of candlelight across her bare skin, he stalked back to their bed and pinched out two flames. Gently, he pressed her backward onto soft white wool.

Light and shadow danced across the delicate curves of her breasts, highlighting the jut of tight and eager nipples. Lower, light shimmered across the gentle slope of her stomach and disappeared into the curls at the apex of her thighs. Kissing her deeply, he let his hands roam freely, taking note of what made her gasp, moan or catch her lower lip between her teeth.

Her own fingers investigated the planes and grooves of his body. And when he could take no more, he slid between her soft thighs and explored the wonders of slow friction, then chased the wild delight of speed as chemistry ignited between them.

Soon after, finding he needed little time for recovery in her presence, he flipped her onto her belly and launched another expedition that ended in a vigorous climb to new heights.

Temporarily sated, he rolled onto his side, taking her with him—her back to his chest—and drew a blanket over them to trap the impressive amount of heat they'd generated. "Why did I turn down your offer that long ago night?" He stroked the curve of her shoulder. "Because one night will never be enough."

"No, it won't." A soft exhale escaped her lips, one that rode on a wave of dismay. Not the hoped-for response. As his touch hadn't disappointed, it must be his words. He'd pushed when he ought to have set her free.

After years of watching her avoid marriage despite the multiple high-ranking offers for her hand, he'd begun to believe he might have a chance. Nearby, a silver twist of a ring burned a hole in the pouch attached to his belt.

But there was something about the tenor of her voice that made him throw aside his carefully prepared words, instead asking, "What's wrong? What aren't you saying?"

"My parents have brokered a contract with Úlfarr Loftandisson."

He let out a slow hiss between his teeth. The thought of anyone else claiming her made his chest tighten and burn. He wanted her more than he'd ever dared admit. "Already?" Only a handful of weeks past the dissolution of her engagement with Val. Yet Dýri wasn't surprised. Úlfarr's family was wealthy and powerful. Sóllilja's father would have leapt at the chance to merge their bloodlines.

She snorted. "Yesterday, Mother sent my trousseau to Reykjavik, to the king's palace. Tomorrow evening is the official engagement ceremony." Rolling in his arms, she tipped her face up to kiss the edge of his jaw. Her fingers danced along his rib cage, inviting more intimacy. "Which is why I can only promise you this moment. Here. Now." She nipped his chin.

"Stop." He drew back and planted the flat of his hand against her breastbone, the mood soured. "You *agreed* to this engagement?" Offense stabbed at his chest. "Am I nothing more than an itch to scratch?"

She huffed. Dismissal flickered in her eyes. "As if you've any interest in relationships. From what I hear, you've a woman in every port. Were you after an extended affair this time?" Frowning, she pulled the blanket to her chest and sat up. "Because I won't throw aside my future for a few days— or even weeks or months—of pleasure."

He froze, incredulous. "So this *is* nothing but a single stolen night?"

"*You* insisted on accompanying *me* to collect the skel-jaskrímsli nacre plates."

"As I recall things, you *invited* me." He propped himself up on an elbow and narrowed his eyes, unashamed of his nakedness. He'd laid his feelings bare, concealed nothing. She was the one who'd withheld pertinent information, treating him like nothing more than an amusing toy, easily abandoned. "Because it's *our* project."

"What do you want from me, Dýri?" Lips pressed flat, she tugged a shirt over her head, then grabbed her trousers. "It's not as if you've ever given me the slightest encouragement before tonight. Not so much as a single sultry look and —" she jabbed a finger at him, "the one time I invited you to my bed, you walked away. Avoided me for weeks. Offered no explanation." She hauled on socks, grabbed her boots. "There's no point in fighting tradition. Am I supposed to apologize for wanting to join my guards in Reykjavik, to travel with the king and his future queen?"

No fight, no fire, no backbone to defy tradition? That wasn't the woman he knew. How could she believe she was out of options? "Since when have you wanted to leave the mountain?"

"Since forever!" Her sharp glare could flay skin. "But Val refused to let me aboard his airship."

"Because your contract, mutually agreed upon, stipulated a wedding first." And because the captain knew Dýri was in love with his fiancée. Afraid she might storm from the cave into the cold night, he dragged on his own shirt and reached for his trousers. "You don't need to marry Úlfarr to—"

"Yes, I do. The humans and their archaic values will not allow an unmarried woman to mingle with their guards. Even wed, I'll be forced to swallow a bitter pill and pretend he's the one in charge."_Her eyes narrowed as her hands curled into fists.

There she was, the woman he loved.

Socks and boots forgotten, he dropped to one knee. So much for a quiet, candlelit proposal with her naked in his arms. But if he could turn this conversation around— "Then marry me instead."

She snorted without looking in his direction, his earnest words not given the slightest bit of weight. "There's little chance the council would appoint you as head guardsman."

"Because I'm part troll?"

"Well, now that you mention it, yes." She pursed her lips

and looped her belt around her waist. "Particularly with the recent battle still fresh in everyone's minds, no matter how bravely you fought."

A point he couldn't argue against. "Does it have to be Reykjavik and the king's court?"

She slid her blade into its sheath and rested her hand on its hilt. "What's the alternative?" Her resigned words carried a sting of resentment. "Stay home polishing boots and sharpening swords while all the other guards don nacreweft armor and embark on grand adventures to seek glory, danger and saga-worthy stories?"

"Fly away with me." There was little else he could offer her. Any status and wealth he'd accumulated wouldn't compare to the intergenerational wealth of Úlfarr's family. "Join the airship's crew."

"And do what? Swab decks?"

He rolled his eyes. "Do whatever you want. Stop working for others—work for yourself. Perfect nacreweft and sell it. Offer the huldufólk first right of refusal. Then we'll form that private security company you always talked about."

"You'd let me run it?" She tipped her head, suspicious.

"Be the muscle that backs you up? Happily." He held out his hand and beckoned with his fingers. "Come back to bed and we'll—" The moon had risen. When had the snowstorm stopped? He pinched out the candle.

"Dýri?"

"Shh."

CHAPTER SIX

Óllilja shoved away all distracting thoughts and emotions, letting her eyes adjust to the dark.

It was in that short space of time she realized the wind no longer howled. Not that the night was quiet. From the cave, she could make out the distant sounds of waves frothing upon the shore. A gull that ought not be awake shrieked once, then fell silent. A stone clattered down the hillside. Closer, the creak of leather. Footsteps?

Snatching up her sword, she darted into a shadow.

Dýri pulled on his boots and threw his belt across his shoulders. He grabbed his battle axe and positioned himself behind a rock outcropping.

"The smell of smoke gave you away." A deep voice mocked them. "Difficult, yes, to scent over the wet rot of those shell monster armored plates you so conveniently packed for me. Perhaps I ought to order my men back to the ship with such a convenient loot and disappear into the night, but recent events suggest I'd be remiss as a cryptid hunter, were I to overlook an opportunity to determine if the myths about Iceland's elves and trolls hold any truths."

Frigg and Hel. Lúgubre and his crew must have been closer than they suspected if they'd sighted the airship when it slowed over Reynisfjara beach, dropping them quickly as they stood atop the crates lashed to their sled.

Woosh. A lit torch landed on the cave floor. So much for moving the shell monster away from the shoreline.

Framed in the entrance stood a man—tall and broad-shouldered, his face half-obscured by shadow. He smiled. A sliver of cunning teeth that held no warmth. A gleaming curved saber at his hip.

"I'm certain you're far more interesting alive than dead, Dýri," Lúgubre called. "Did you fight with the trolls or the huldufólk in the recent battle? The latter, I suspect. Oh, the tales you might tell—and I have men interested in making you talk. Much as I miss that House Nissi, the pair of you are worth far more on the black market. Even if you're missing a few non-crucial body parts." He paused. "Last chance for a peaceful surrender."

A chill crawled through her as the meaning of his words settled. The Spaniard didn't intend to kill them. He meant to cage them—to sell them to collectors who considered non-human sentient beings to be curiosities, creatures without rights, valued for education or entertainment. Or as a means to glean information in yet another attempt to undermine the Kingdom of Iceland.

Dýri caught her eye, tipped his head, directing her gaze

to the torch. A dark, choking smoke poured forth from the flames. Already visibility was compromised. Soon they would be forced out.

"No?" The man clucked his tongue. "So be it." He waved the men hovering behind him forward. "Grab them!"

Past experience dictated that they would attempt to subdue Dýri first. A moment she would work to her advantage. Sure enough, two crewmen rushed toward him with a net stretched between them, mesh that glinted in the firelight. Wired cording? Best not to find out.

They were fast, but she was faster.

With a single merciless lunge, she sliced through one man's hamstring. His leg buckled as he crashed to the ground howling, the net twisting in his grip and throwing the second attacker off balance.

Which was when Dýri seized his moment. Running in a low crouch, he slammed his shoulder into the other man's chest, driving him further into the cave, twisting the net into a shimmering cable while wrapping it around the man's throat.

"Look out!" he cried.

But she didn't turn fast enough. An arrow struck her in the shoulder with a sickening thud. She slumped against the cave wall, dropping her sword. Pain flared, white-hot. *Helvíti!* Where was an archer positioned that he could do such precise damage?

"*¡Carajo!* Alive, I said!" Lúgubre ordered, boots crunching on stone as he strode into the cavern, through the smoke. Only the slightest of limps hinted that he'd not won every battle he fought. She intended to add today to his list of failures.

Biting back a cry, she forced herself into motion, reaching for her blade before—

Too late.

A rough hand wrapped around her wrist, yanking her backward, twisting her arm behind her back. "No need for that, sweetheart," the Spaniard hissed into her ear. "Pretty thing, aren't you? Or you will be. Customers generally prefer a clean cryptid."

She threw her head backward to smash the man's nose, to crack his jaw, anything to loosen his grip, but he evaded her efforts with surprising ease, his limp of little impediment. A boot slammed on the backs of her legs, dropping her to her knees. Muscle and tendon screamed as shackles clamped down upon her wrists, locking her arms behind her. He snapped off the fletching, but left the rest of the arrow embedded in her shoulder.

Lúgubre yanked her to her feet and spun her about—in time to watch an arrow lodge in Dýri's knee. One that hissed and sparked. Several men lay bleeding and motionless at his feet and his battle axe glistened with blood, but it was the potassium-tipped weapon—tröllabaniör, a weapon known to stop trolls—that provided the Spaniard's crew with the tiniest sliver of surprise. A moment that lasted long enough for a second wire mesh net to tangle his arms.

"No!" Her scream was a futile protest against fate as more men rushed in, this time with ropes and chains and a hinged circlet of steel.

Dýri hacked at the net, his motions frenzied and ineffectual, if worrisome enough to forestall the crew's efforts to bind him.

The sharp edge of a knife bit into her neck. "Drop your weapon, troll. Before I decide the profit off your fae woman is not worth my time or trouble."

"If you let her go," Dýri growled through gritted teeth as he lowered his axe, "I'll come quietly."

"As if you're in any position to negotiate terms." Lúgubre laughed, then barked orders at his men. "Collar him and secure a chain. March him down the hill like the animal he is. Don't forget the battle axe. A troll's weapon ought to bring a good price." With a hand between her shoulders, he shoved Sóllilja out into the cold night, onto the steep path that led down the hill.

Hot tears rolled down her cheeks. The pain in her shoulder and feet faded into insignificance as a dark void opened inside her. For years she'd denied herself any real hope of a life with Dýri, convinced such fantasies were foolish and impossible. Tonight, he'd shattered that resolve with a few simple words. He'd offered her marriage. A different future. One that they alone shaped. Together.

And before she could grasp that future—before she could even believe it was possible—this Spanish cryptid hunter threatened to snuff it out. She trembled. From blood loss. From rage. From the unbearable possibility that their freedom might be lost forever.

No. She refused to accept that future. There must be a way to gain the upper hand. As she stumbled down the rock-studded icy path, she scanned the night horizon. At the edge of the water, the Spaniard's crew wrestled with the crates filled with the skeljaskrímsli's scales. Determined thieves. A problem, but not an immediate one.

There.

On the rocky outcropping near where they'd stowed their crates, a glint of metal flashed. An archer stood, poised with line of sight into the cave from across the snowy landscape that stretched between the two. Not that distant, but there was the matter of her injured shoulder, bound wrists and the armed men that lay between them.

If she could eliminate him as a threat... All she needed was opportunity. Which came at the base of the hill when Lúgubre shoved her into the arms of one of his men. "Leave the arrow in place. Haul her to the ship and tell the doctor to repair the damage."

A mistake, removing the threat of instant death from her throat. For it provided her with the chance to glance over her shoulder, to assess Dýri's location: halfway down the hillside, led by a chain hooked to a padlocked iron collar. Blood stained his pant leg from knee to boot. Several silver-tipped spears were aimed at his backside, but he took no notice. The fire of a warrior burned in his eyes. He would fight. They would fight. And gods help anyone who stood in their path.

She tossed a glance at the archer standing upon the hillock and raised her eyebrows. His chin lifted, and the slightest of nods encouraged her to act.

With a whispered appeal to Týr, she clenched her teeth against the pain that ripped through her shoulder and shot her leg out in a swift arc, catching her captor by the ankles and sweeping his feet from under him. Before he even hit the ground, she was chasing after the man holding Dýri's battle axe. A kick to his back sent him sprawling in the snow, the weapon far from his grasp. Not that she could pick it up. A boot to the side of his head ensured he wouldn't either.

An arrow thwacked into the ground beside her.

Behind her, Dýri roared his anger, but there was no helping him. Not with an archer taking aim. Zigging and zagging, she ran across the uneven ground as more arrows embedded themselves in the snow-covered field, unable—or unwilling—to drop a moving target.

She hit the base of the hill and scrambled up the sloped backside of the volcanic stone at full speed, growling at the man notching another arrow into his crossbow.

"Stop!" he yelled, eyes wide with terror. "Please. You're to be taken alive, not—"

His final words were cut off when she plowed into him, headfirst, and with enough force to hurl him backward over the rocky ridge and onto the ground at the base of the cliff. Men yelled and ran to his broken body, but were unable to rouse him.

She turned and dropped her arse into the snow, sucking in deep gulps of air, struggling to breathe through the torment that was her shoulder while watching a fight unfold at the base of the cave.

Dýri had broken free and turned his chain into a weapon. Spinning it in his hand, he marched forward, cutting through Lúgubre's men with startling ease. His grandmother would be proud. *She* was proud. He would make the most magnificent of life partners. Those men who did not fall scattered, running like the cowards they were, until only the Spaniard stood upon the plain, saber raised and gleaming coldly in the moonlight.

Stopping only to retrieve his battle axe, Dýri advanced upon his nemesis.

"Stop!" The hunter stepped backward, spreading his arms. "Enough damage has been done. You've more than proven yourself. Negotiations are in order. Half the profits? Second in command of my ship?"

Dýri didn't bother to acknowledge the parley. "Never chain a troll." Rage contorted his face. "Not that you'll ever have a chance to apply the lesson. Drop your sword and I'll grant you a merciful death."

Lúgubre lunged. But Dýri's bulk was deceiving. He dodged the man's blade, dropping into a crouch to hack into the Spaniard's ankle.

Blood poured from the man's boot, staining the white snow. But he limped forward, intent upon winning, though he would only end up dying by degrees.

"Surrender," Dýri ordered.

"Never!" The hunter reached inside his coat, pulled out a knife, and sent it flying.

Though he spun away, the blade lodged in Dýri's side.

Sóllilja gasped and jumped to her feet, ready to run to him.

But the injury didn't slow him at all. He whipped the chain around and yanked the Spaniard's other leg from beneath him. As Lúgubre fell, he advanced, battle axe raised high. As the other man rolled away, the killing blow descended. Except Dýri brought the cutting edge down upon the hunter's wrist, severing the hand that gripped his saber.

The Spaniard's scream echoed through the night. Until Dýri struck him with the handle of his axe, rendering him unconscious.

Crewmen who had paused to stare at the unfolding scene turned and ran for the inlet, for the boats they'd dragged ashore. There, men still struggled to drag the crates of shell monster scales, managing to move them only a few inches at a time. Arguments broke out. Some seeming to wish to depart with speed, others recognizing the opportunity that a fallen captain presented and ordered efforts to load the crates to continue.

On the field, Dýri yanked the knife from his side and threw it to the ground. He produced a key ring from Lúgubre's pocket and freed himself from the iron collar, clamping it about the Spaniard's neck instead. She watched, awestruck, as he lifted the hunter's saber, expecting him to end the man's life. Instead, he drove the tip through a link of the chain into the frozen ground, pinning him in place.

CHAPTER SEVEN

The blinding rage that gripped Dýri began to dissipate, leaving behind a deadly calm. Lúgubre's chest still rose and fell, but not for long. The man who'd trafficked cryptids, selling their parts and their young on the black market, would never do so again.

He strode away, abandoning the man to die alone. Let him wake upon the frozen ground to pain and panic. If fear didn't stop his heart, blood loss and hypothermia would drain the last of his life soon enough. Either was justice.

This miserable excuse for a man had nearly ruined everything. His woman was badly injured. Enough so that her valiant efforts had taken everyone but him by surprise, providing him with the opening he needed to save them both *and* call the Spaniard to account. Her strength and determination made his heart ache with admiration.

And love.

He took the slope two steps at a time, eyes fixed on her form at the cliff's edge. "How bad is your shoulder?" He knelt behind her to free her wrists from the shackles that bound them, keeping his emotions firmly in check. Triage first.

"Bad." Her face was pale, her expression strained. Every beat of her heart must throb in her shoulder. "But nothing that won't heal. Or prevent a wedding."

His heart stopped, then took off at a gallop. Had he heard her clearly? "Is that an acceptance?"

She grabbed his shaking hand and pressed his palm to her face. "It is. I've only ever wanted you. When I thought you didn't feel the same, I tried to move on. To set you free. But I can't. The thought of being separated from you again —" She swallowed. "I want a future with you and only you."

"Even with my heritage?" His gut twisted, but he needed to hear her answer.

"It's a part of who you are, but it changes nothing." She pressed a fast kiss to his lips. "Now, if you could remove this arrow from my shoulder so we can stop Lúgubre's crew from making off with the nacre plates and plan a wedding..."

Pride swelled in his chest, sharp and sweet. "A warrior through and through, no matter what your parents wished you to become."

"And soon to be your wife."

A smile pulled at his lips. "And my bride." He pulled a medical kit from a pouch at his belt. "Now hold still." He wrapped a fist around the arrowhead protruding from her shoulder and drew what remained of the arrow through her flesh.

She hissed at the pain, frowned at the blood that streamed down her arm. "Bind it. Fast."

A splash of ethanol drained the last of the blood from her face. He steadied her as she fought a wave of dizziness, then produced gauze pads and linen strips. "Lift your arm." He pressed a pad to the entry wound, hating every moment of pain she suffered. "Hold this." And another to the exit wound. With a few deft maneuvers, her shoulder was bound tight.

Relief surged through him. The damage was minimal.

"How are you uninjured?" She tugged at his shirt, lifting the hem to stare at the red welt made by the Spaniard's hard-thrown knife.

"When Lúgubre arrived with his men, there was no time to do more than sling my belt over my shoulder." His knife had cut a gash into the leather pouch attached to his belt. He tugged out her ruined nålbound glove. "The nacreweft deflected his blade."

She gaped, then grinned. "You kept it."

At the water's edge, she'd tossed aside the torn glove in her haste to rinse the shell monster's blood from her wound. He'd picked it up when she wasn't looking. And it had saved him.

"I did." With a fingertip, he closed her mouth. "Think about it later." His words were gentle. Much as he wanted to kiss her, to drag her back to the cave and celebrate skin to skin, there were loose ends to tie up. "First things first. We need to retain the means to make far more nacreweft armor than a single pair of gloves."

Perched on the side of a sloped volcanic stone, they took in the chaotic scene below them.

No need to chase anyone away as not a single man had ventured across the field to Lúgubre's side. To stem the bleeding. To pull the sword from the ground. To drag his body back to their ship. No, they were too intent upon securing profit by making off with the hard work of others.

Not that the Spaniard's crew had made much progress. Looking from their rocky ridge toward the inlet, Dýri could see his plan had worked. Men pushed and pulled at the sled loaded with crates of skeljaskrímsli scales while others argued, pointing at the water and throwing hands in the air.

"We were going nowhere but up, so I slashed the skid buoys." Dýri shot his fiancée a sly glance. She'd forgive his bragging. "Carrying each crate—ones loaded with the strength of a troll—down the shore to their own boats is a Herculean task. They'll have to repack each one. It'll take the humans hours."

"Smart. And a touch devious." Her eyes gleamed with admiration. "I like that about you."

He drew her back down behind the ridge, taking what shelter they could. "Then you'll like this next part even more. You cannot fight." He touched a finger to her lips when she drew breath to protest. "Even I am outnumbered. But I have a plan."

He unhooked the drinking horn from his belt, lifted his

axe and—with a single blow—cut off its tip, rendering it hollow.

"You mean to scare them off? By suggesting another shell monster might be nearby?"

"I do." Smart, his future wife. He winked, then brought the horn to his lips.

A long, low, raw sound rippled into the night. Caught up by the wind, tossed against rocks and muffled by the dead winter grass, its origins were impossible to pinpoint.

"Did you hear that?" A hoarse whisper from one of the men below.

Sóllilja grinned at him.

He drew another deep breath and blew. This time the sound emerged as a guttural groan. Hungry. As if some giant beast stalked nearby, monstrous and merciless, mourning the death of one of its own.

Panicked voices erupted, words in a number of languages, all tangling together in fear. He caught the whole of a single agitated sentence. "Another monster approaches!"

Excellent.

Dýri placed his mouth to the war horn and blew again, building the sound, twisting the cries to ever higher pitches. Then, abruptly, he stopped.

A moment Sóllilja punctuated by rolling a rock down the steep face of the outcropping.

More blasts from the horn. Short and truncated now. Each time Dýri drew breath, she tossed another rock.

"Over there!" Then a sharp scream cut through the night. "Shell monster!"

What? A second creature? Had a skeljaskrímsli come looking for its mate?

Wide-eyed, they caught each other's gaze.

Panicked shouts filled the air. There were clunks and thuds, scrapes and clangs, clatters and splashes. Confused, chaotic sounds.

Carefully, they peered over the ridge again and watched three hooked claws haul a rowboat down into the black water of the inlet. Its passengers swam for shore, kicking and splashing and shouting. But one by one, the unseen creature moving beneath the surface caught them and dragged them under. None resurfaced.

"Did we accidentally summon a skeljaskrímsli?" Sóllilja breathed.

"I believe so," he answered, unable to look away.

The creature's head emerged first—blazing red eyes framed by dark, dense scales. Then its humped bulk followed, stalking onto land. With a throaty bellow—not unlike the call of the horn itself—the shell monster bared its teeth and charged.

Those men possessing firearms opened fire, but the bullets glanced harmlessly off the creature's armored plates, the ricochets only enraging it further. The wiser sailors turned and fled for their boats, rowing hard, oars biting into the black water. Escaping while the creature attacked those on shore.

One man was crushed underfoot. Another's scream cut short as his throat was torn open. The monster's clubbed tail swept sideways, shattering skulls and splintering bones.

Chaos dissolved into silence—save for the wet crunch of the creature finishing its grim work.

The skeljaskrímsli lumbered toward the crates that held the remains of its fellow creature. It lowered its head, sniffed, and let out a sound that froze Dýri's blood—a low, keening wail of pain and fury.

Then it fell silent. Turned. Sniffed the wind.

"Help!" A cry all but whipped away by the wind.

Lúgubre.

Frigg and Hel. He yanked Sóllilja below the ridge, wrapped his arms about her. "Don't move. Don't make a sound."

"Someone—please!" The hunter's voice broke, desperate now.

Another guttural howl cut through the night. Snow crunched beneath heavy feet as the creature crossed the plain, its glowing eyes locking on the staked man.

It circled him once. Twice. Snorting. Testing. Lúgubre's terror turned to ragged sobs. Sóllilja squeezed his hand. Dýri had intended a slow, cold death for the Spaniard, though this was a more fitting end. The man deserved a death dealt to him by tooth and claw, yet it was no easy thing to watch.

The creature threw its head back and a scream of fury tore from its throat. Then it lunged, sinking its long dagger-like teeth deep into the hunter's abdomen. With a brutal wrench, it tore him free of the sword that pinned him to the ground, swung its massive head, and ran—with surprising speed despite its bulk—across the snow.

They watched, silent, as the shell monster vanished

toward the black sand beach, its burden limp between its jaws. Then nothing but the hiss of the wind remained.

They sagged into each other. Cold and wounded. But alive.

THEY'D DEFEATED THEIR ENEMY, called a monster from the deep. Watched the skeljaskrímsli destroy everything in its path. Survived it all.

No courtly tea, no embroidered gown, no parade of guards had ever made her feel this *alive*. This wild edge between life and death was where she belonged. Heart pounding, lungs burning. The grit and the grime. The danger, the chaos. Blood and fear and the ache of survival.

This. She wanted *this*. Heart pounding, lungs burning, every inch of her buzzing with life. And she wanted it with Dýri.

Not just the work. Not just the fight. But everything that came after as well. Their bodies tangled, bare and trembling, locked together with raw, skin-to-skin honesty. Equals in life, both in and out of bed.

"You're thinking too hard." His voice was a low rumble against her ear as he shifted to face her. A hint of worry tugged at his features. "Change your mind? Settling for the certainty of Reykjavik over a life of risking it all?"

"Not even for a moment." Fisting the collar of his tunic, she dragged him close, rolling until his weight settled over her. Her shoulder protested, but the pain only proved she was still here, still breathing. That this was real. That Dýri was *hers*. "But we need to fund this venture you've proposed. Nacreweft is ours alone. Only we know the secret of a successful weave. If we offer it to the council, to the huldufólk for a hefty sum—"

"First right of refusal." He smiled against her lips. "But retain the rights for personal use. And for any additional guards in our employ." He kissed her, slow and sure. "You've a brilliant mind."

A compliment that warmed her almost as much as his body heat. "If they decline?"

He shrugged. "A bidding war erupts. Either way, we win."

A faint glimmer of light crept across the sky. Soon their ride would arrive, but she didn't want to return home. Not yet. Not unless... "Would your mother be angry if she missed your wedding today?"

Dýri blinked. "Today?"

"Here." Her fingers trailed over the sharp angle of his jaw, down the column of his throat. "On the beach."

"Not so long as I bring you home as my bride." He kissed her again. Softly at first. Then deeper. Heat rose between them despite the cold air and the scent of salt and blood. He drew back, his gaze dark and searching. "You're certain?"

"More than." Her voice caught. "I want this—us— freedom and love, battle and rest. No pretending. No hiding who I am." She pushed her hips against his, drawing a pained moan. "You're my rock, the blade at my back, and the only person who makes me want to lower my guard."

"Especially after a good fight?" The corner of his mouth kicked up. He thrust against her. "On the hill? In the snow? Alone beneath the wide-open sky?"

She nipped his chin. "Yes."

Stripped of all pretense, they sought each other with ragged breaths and shaking hands. Not to forget what had happened, but because they were alive, and they were together.

Standing on black sand with a backdrop of basalt columns and wave-splashed sea stacks, Dýri's breath caught as he listened to the only woman he'd ever loved speak vows that bound her to him, words he'd nearly stopped fighting to hear.

A moment he'd only dared dream about was finally real.

The galleon had disappeared beyond the horizon. The crates were loaded aboard the airship. All evidence of their presence erased from the cave. At the insistence of their friends, they'd washed and dressed in wedding finery. Someone had braided a circle of flowers for Sóllilja's hair and found them both fur cloaks.

His heart gave a great thud as he lifted a silver ring from his blade and slid it onto her finger. A promise that he would always fight for her. In turn, she reached up with steady hands to tie a leather cord about his neck, one from which Thor's hammer hung, pressing the amulet to his chest, a gesture entreating the god's protection.

Their friend Hildur's voice rose in a low chant, invoking

blessings from the gods, words carried skyward by the offshore winds. She thrust a drinking horn full of mead into his hand and commanded them to seal the oath. He held the horn to his bride's lips, then his, each letting the honeyed liquid warm their throats.

Then their eyes locked as love blazed between them.

Married at last.

ABOUT THE AUTHOR

Though ANNE RENWICK holds a Ph.D. in biology and greatly enjoyed tormenting the overburdened undergraduates who were her students, fiction has always been her first love. Today, she writes steampunk romance, placing a new kind of biotech in the hands of mad scientists, proper young ladies and determined villains.

Anne brings an unusual perspective to steampunk. A number of years spent locked inside the bowels of a biological research facility left her permanently altered. In her steampunk world, the Victorian fascination with all things anatomical led to a number of alarming biotechnological advances. Ones that the enemies of Britain would dearly love to possess.

www.AnneRenwick.com

instagram.com/anne_renwick

facebook.com/AnneRenwickAuthor

pinterest.com/AuthorAnneRenwick